This book belongs to

....

For all parents and children
who love reading together

Ferdinand Fox's Big Sleep

Copyright Karen Inglis 2012
Published by Well Said Press 2012
83 Castelnau, London, SW13 9RT, England

ISBN: 978-0-9569323-5-8

~WS~
Well Said Press

www.wellsaidpress.com

To Isabella
Best wishes!   Karen

Ferdinand Fox's
Big Sleep

Karen Inglis
Illustrated by Damir Kundalić

Ferdinand Fox curled up in the sun

as the church of St Mary struck quarter past one.

His tummy was full, he was ready for sleep,

and closing his eyes he began to count sheep.

Within a few moments he started to snore,
his tail wrapped around him, his chin on his paw.
As he fell into slumber he started to dream
of sausages, hamburgers, cakes and ice cream.

Peter Maceever who lived in Fife Way

was working at home doing business that day.

As he rose from his desk and looked to his lawn

he spotted a bundle, all gingery fawn.

'By Jove!' said Maceever. 'Just what can that be?

It can't be a cat. It looks bigger to me.'

He picked up his camera and peered through the zoom.

Ferdinand now looked close to his room.

'It's a fox!' he cried, 'come out of the wild!
He thinks he's alone here!' Maceever smiled.

'He obviously thinks my garden's the wood.
His den must be in the neighbourhood.'

Peter Maceever stole out of his house

and crept down the path, as quiet as a mouse.

He tipped on his tiptoes. He held back a cough.

At the slightest of sounds the fox would run off.

Ferdinand Fox continued to snore,
dreaming of chocolate and cream buns galore!

Maceever moved closer. The fox was in view.

St Mary's church clock struck half-past two.

Maceever waited, then let out a cough.

The fox didn't wake, and it didn't run off!

Maceever was worried. He scratched his head.

Could it be that this fox was dead?

The clock struck three. He tiptoed to check.

The fox lay snoring, the sun on its neck!

'I'll take a quick picture - only the one.

When he hears the click he'll be off at a run!'

At the sound of the camera Ferdinand stirred

as his dreamy blancmange began to go blurred.

With a sigh and a yawn he opened his eyes
to two long legs stretched up to the skies.

Ferdinand lazily peered at this sight

but was far too sleepy to contemplate flight.

He lifted his paw and scratched at his cheek…

…then closed his eyes and went straight back to sleep!

Peter Maceever strolled back to his house,

no longer creeping as quiet as a mouse.

Ferdinand dreamed on, of lamb and coleslaw.

The church of St Mary struck quarter to four.

St Mary's struck five. A breeze stirred the air.

Maceever yawned and rose from his chair.

The sun had moved down, the shadows were long
and the fox that had slept in the garden – was gone.

Stories for older children
by Karen Inglis

The Secret Lake

A 'time-slip' mystery adventure
for 8-11 year-olds.
In print and e-book - 5-Star reviews
www.thesecretlake.com

Eeek! The Runaway Alien

A fast-paced story about a runaway alien who loves
soccer! Age 7-10 years.
Fun black and white illustrations!
In print and e-book - 5-Star reviews
www.eeekthealien.com

Coming soon...!

Ferdinand Fox and the Hedgehog
Ferdinand Fox and the Lost Boy
Ferdinand Fox and the Break-in
Ferdinand Fox, the Kittens and the Alley Monster
Ferdinand Fox and the Close Shave

Find out more and sign up for sneak previews at:

ferdinandfox.co.uk

facebook.com/ferdinandfoxadventures